# Alice's Adventures
# Under Ground

# ALICE'S ADVENTURES UNDER GROUND

BY

LEWIS CARROLL

PAVILION

Published in association with the British Library

This edition first published
in Great Britain in 1985
by Pavilion Books Limited
London House, Great Eastern Wharf
Parkgate Road, London SW11 4NQ

Fifth impression 2000

The photographs are reproduced with the kind permission
of Christ Church College Library, Oxford. The National
Portrait Gallery, London and Graham Ovenden Esq.

*Alice's Adventures Under Ground*
is British Library Add Ms 46.700.

Edited by Russell Ash

Printed and bound in Spain by Mondadori

British Library Cataloguing in Publication Data

Carroll, Lewis
    Alice's adventures under-ground.
    Rn: Charles Lutwidge Dodgson    1. Title
    823'.8[J]    PZ7

    ISBN 1-85145-4713
    D.L. TO: 1301-2000

# CONTENTS

*Lewis Carroll's photograph of Alice which formerly
concealed his drawing of her on the last page of his book.*

# FOREWORD
## by Mary Jean St Clair, Alice's Granddaughter

When the stories that make up this book were told to my grand-mother by Charles Dodgson (the real name of 'Lewis Carroll'), she was a little girl living in the Deanery at Christ Church, Oxford. When she died aged 82 in 1934, at Westerham in Kent, the legend of Alice still haunted her. On her death the national Press compared her with Beatrice, Laura, Stella and other women made immortal by contact with literary genius, famous for being a little girl to whom a shy, clever don had enjoyed telling fairy tales.

Sadly, I don't remember her, as she died when I was a baby, but she loved children, and the entries in her diary for the times that I was taken to stay with her show what pleasure these visits gave her.

Her childhood in Oxford was a happy one and she and her brothers and sisters were very close to their parents, especially their father, Dean Liddell. A great treat for the children was to go riding with their father, and for this special pleasure, which they took in turns, they would consult his diary which always lived by the fireplace in his study, to fix a time for a ride between his engagements for the day.

As they rode in Bagley Wood and Wytham Park, their father would point out the different forest trees and the patterns of the clouds and shadows and other interesting aspects of the countryside. Perhaps because of this, Alice always loved any-thing to do with wild flowers, animals and natural history. On one of these rides, Alice's pony crossed its legs and fell, breaking Alice's hip. Dean Liddell had to leave her lying by the roadside while he went to get help; she was rescued by some passers-by, who put her on a mattress on the back of their cart and took her back to Oxford.

It was soon after the Liddells had come to Oxford from Westminster in 1855 that Charles Dodgson first saw the children. He went to the Deanery to help his friend Reginald Southey take a photograph of Christ Church Cathedral, and they were playing in the garden. Their first contacts were in fact made through his hobby of photography, and a rather unsuccessful attempt to teach Henry Liddell his sums. The children, especially Alice, became his favourite photographic subjects, and many charming photographs exist that were taken at that time.

The Liddells had a house at Llandudno where they went for their summer holidays. There is no evidence in Dodgson's diaries that he visited them there, but I have in an album of photographs taken by Dodgson one of the house, *Penmorfa*, with the children sitting on the garden steps. So, if this photograph was indeed taken by Dodgson, it is proof that he did go there and no doubt continued his storytelling while walking on the Great Orme. There is even a statue of the White Rabbit at Llandudno to commemorate *Alice in Wonderland*.

Although Alice was Dodgson's favourite and the main inspiration for his stories, her two sisters, Lorina and Edith, were included in the storytelling and on the boat trips when they would all plead with him to tell them more. So it was a sadness to all the family, and no doubt to Dodgson too, when Edith died in 1876 aged 22, just before she was to be married. It had a very profound effect on Alice, and although there were rumours that Prince Leopold, Queen Victoria's son, and indeed Dodgson himself, wished to marry her, it was said that because of the shock of Edith's death she waited until 1880 before marrying Reginald Hargreaves.

After Alice grew up, there was very little contact between her and Dodgson. A certain coolness became apparent between him and the Dean and Mrs Liddell who perhaps disapproved of his possible interest in marrying Alice. She was just seventeen when he photographed her for the last time. Alice asked Dodgson to be godfather to a son, but he refused, and the only letter I have from Dodgson to Alice after she was married is a formal note asking her to tea when she was visiting the Deanery for the last time. During the middle period of Alice's life she was not much affected by the Dodgson relationship, but as she grew older and the *Alice* books gained increasing fame, she became an object of curiosity. Usually this embarrassed her: 'I went to a meeting yesterday and after it was over the lady who addressed us came up and said, "I must shake hands with the real Alice," and after a few inane remarks she asked, "Did you know Mr Dodgson?" Well, I ask you . . .'

Alice had always kept the manuscript of her adventures in Wonderland and when she moved it had gone with her to *Cuffnells*, in the New Forest. There it lay for years, on a table in an ante-room, with apparently no particular care being taken of it until 1928.

My grandfather's death in that year meant that money had to be found to pay death duties. The family thought of things they could sell to raise the required amount, and eventually decided on the *Alice* manuscript, the most valuable item they possessed. Sotheby's suggested a reserve of only £4,000. In the event it fetched £15,400, an enormous amount for those days, and went to America.

During the auction, Alice was in the limelight again, and the Press had a marvellous time photographing 'the real Alice' and making up stories about the poor, childless, widowed lady, who was having to let her country house to make ends meet. My father, one of her sons, would not have been too pleased at this invention, as he was very much alive, and busily collecting copies of the various editions of *Alice*. When he died he left no fewer than 250 different versions.

In 1932, when she was eighty, Alice undertook her last engagement on behalf of Wonderland. She was invited to New York on the centenary of Dodgson's birth to attend the celebrations, and to receive an Honorary Degree from Columbia University. For an elderly lady, accustomed to a quiet life, this must have been quite a revolution! There were Press receptions, police escorts through New York, a suite at the Waldorf Astoria, a film and a radio broadcast—all very daunting for an old lady to face. There are two books full of Press cuttings from the visit. She sailed back on the *Aquitania* flying a special Cheshire Cat flag, much to the embarrassment of the Captain.

After the visit to New York there were many letters and requests for autographs and a few for personal appearances, but by this time Alice was becoming exhausted by the demands of her fame. She wrote to her son, 'But, oh, my dear, I am tired of being Alice in Wonderland. Does it sound ungrateful? It is—only I do get tired!'

While she was ill, her decline was reported every day in the newspapers and in the *Daily Telegraph* list of 'notable invalids'. Her death made headlines in national newspapers. Strange fame perhaps for one who had done little to deserve it, but without whose inspiration and persuasion one of the most famous books in the world would never have been written.

*Alice aged 80, on her visit to New York.*

# INTRODUCTION
## The Story Of *Alice's Adventures Under Ground*

The germ of *Alice* was an extensive story, told in a boat to the 3 children of Dean Liddell: it was afterwards, at the request of Miss Alice Liddell, written out for her, in MS [manuscript] print, with pen-and-ink pictures (*such* pictures!) of my own devising: without the least idea, at the time, that it would ever be published. But friends urged me to print it, so it was re-written, and enlarged, and published.

So wrote the author of *Alice in Wonderland* to a friend a hundred years ago and twenty years after it was first published. But although the book was to become perhaps the best-known children's story of all time, the manuscript he referred to—*Alice's Adventures Under Ground*—upon which it was based, is less familiar.

The story of *Alice's Adventures Under Ground* began on 4 July 1862. On that summer's day five people set out in a boat for a picnic on the bank of the river Isis in Oxfordshire. Three of them were Alice, Lorina and Edith, the young daughters of Henry Liddell, the Dean of Christ Church, Oxford. They were accompanied by two adults, the Rev. Robinson Duckworth and his friend, Charles Lutwidge Dodgson, a young mathematics lecturer at Dean Liddell's college.

Dodgson, who wrote under the pseudonym, 'Lewis Carroll', began to tell a story, or series of stories, in which the main character was one of the girls, Alice Liddell, then aged ten. On this and subsequent trips, the 'interminable fairy-tale', as Carroll described it, developed and Alice pestered him to write it down for her. According to Duckworth, he sat up all night recalling the details as he had related them to the Liddell girls and sketched an initial outline, expanding it on a train journey

*Edith, Lorina and Alice Liddell photographed by Carroll, 1859.*

*Robinson Duckworth, Carroll's
companion on the 'Alice'
boat trip of 1862.*

*Lewis Carroll aged about 24.
A photograph attributed to
Reginald Southey, c.1856.*

to London when he visited the International Exhibition. It went through at least one draft and developed into the tale he called *Alice's Adventures Under Ground*. This he laboriously wrote in a hand that the young Alice would find legible, leaving spaces for thirty-seven illustrations. He completed this task on 10 February 1863, but the pictures proved more difficult, for although Carroll was a contemporary and friend of most of the Pre-Raphaelites, he was the first to admit that his own talents lay in directions other than those of a draughtsman. However, his pictures convey precisely his personal view of how the inhabitants of 'Wonderland' ought to look, and thus have an intimacy not found in the work of subsequent illustrators of his books. He eventually finished the drawings on 13 September 1864 and sent the completed manuscript to a bookbinder, presenting it to Alice on 26 November. Dedicated as 'A Christmas Gift to a Dear Child, in Memory of a Summer Day', she was to treasure it for almost 65 years.

Friends who heard about the story while Carroll was revising it encouraged him to have it published. In doing so, he expanded it considerably (from 12,715 words to 26,211 words) and made many changes from the version he had written as a personal gift for Alice, introducing new elements into the story and having the celebrated *Punch* artist, John Tenniel, produce illustrations more refined than his own.

Having arranged for Tenniel to illustrate the book, Carroll anguished over its title. In a letter to their mutual friend, the dramatist, Tom Taylor, he explained that he feared that *Alice's Adventures Under Ground* might appear to be a book containing 'instruction about mines'; he therefore suggested:

*Alice among the elves/goblins,* or
*Alice's hour/doings/adventures in elf-land/wonderland*

He expressed his personal preference for *Alice's Adventures in Wonderland*, which is what it became—though usually shortened simply to *Alice in Wonderland*.

This version of the story (his original manuscript of which was lost) was published by Macmillan on 4 July 1865—three

*Carroll's last photograph of Alice, c. 1869*

years to the day from when he had started telling it to Alice and her sisters. This edition is now very rare, because, apparently, Tenniel was 'dissatisfied with the printing of the pictures' and all but a few copies were recalled. A satisfactory 'first' edition appeared dated '1866', but was seemingly on sale from late 1865. It was followed in 1871 with Alice's further adventures in *Through the Looking-Glass, and What Alice Found There*. The two books were immediately and hugely successful and have remained so since they were first published. They have been in print in hundreds of editions, in different languages and with the work of numerous illustrators for 120 years; they have been performed on stage, on television and in the cinema, and have been the basis of a veritable 'Alice industry' which persists to the present day.

Carroll himself contributed to this industry: in 1885 he approached Alice Liddell—by now grown up and married to Reginald Hargreaves, and with children of her own—asking if he could borrow his original manuscript in order to prepare a facsimile. This letter, dated 1 March 1885 and now in the Henry W. and Albert A. Berg Collection of the New York Public Library, indicates something of the divide the intervening years had created between them:

My dear Mrs Hargreaves,

I fancy this will come to you almost like a voice from the dead, after so many years of silence—and yet those years have made no difference, that I can perceive, in *my* clearness of memory of the old days when we *did* correspond. I am getting to feel what an old man's failing memory is, as to recent events and new friends (for instance, I made friends, only a few weeks ago, with a very nice little maid of about 12, and had a walk with her—and now I can't recall either of her names!) but my mental picture is as vivid as ever, of one who was, through so many years, my ideal child-friend. I have had scores of child-friends since your time: but they have been quite a different thing.

However, I did not begin this letter to say all *that*. What I want to ask is—would you have any objection to the original MS book of *Alice's Adventures* (which I suppose you still possess) being published in facsimile? The idea of doing so occurred to me only the other day. If, on consideration, you come to the conclusion that you would rather *not* have it done, there is an end to the matter. If, however, you give a favourable reply, I would be much obliged if you would lend it me (registered post I should think would be safest) that I may consider the possibilities. I have not seen it for about 20 years: so am by no means sure that the illustrations may not prove to be so awfully bad, that to reproduce them would be absurd.

There can be no doubt that I should incur the charge of gross egoism in publishing it. But I don't care for that in the least: knowing that I have no such motive: only I think, considering the extraordinary popularity the books have had (we have sold more than 120,000 of the two) there must be many who would like to see the original form.
Always your friend,
C. L. Dodgson

Alice agreed, and Carroll wrote to her again on 7 March 1885, clearly delighted that she still valued his work:

My dear Mrs Hargreaves,
Many thanks for your permission. The greatest care shall be taken of the MS (I am gratified at your making *that* a condition!). My own wishes would be distinctly *against* reproducing the photograph.
Always your friend,
C. L. Dodgson

The photograph he refers to was one he had taken of Alice when she was seven and which was pasted on the last page of the manuscript, and it would seem that both he and Alice had reservations about reproducing such a personal item. Alice then sent the precious manuscript, and Carroll wrote to her on

21 March to thank her. But it was some months before the preparatory work was completed. Carroll insisted on supervising the photographer responsible for copying the pages, a Mr Noad of Eastham, Essex, and perhaps naively agreed to pay him in advance for his work and for the subcontracted work of making the zinc plates from which it was to be printed. After delivering only a handful of the plates, Noad disappeared —apparently on the run from his creditors, and with Carroll's prepayment in his pocket. Carroll returned Alice's manuscript to her on 18 October 1885 and was reluctant to borrow it again, leaving himself no choice but to pursue the dilatory Mr Noad. Although the facsimile was intended to have been published for Christmas 1885, the vanishing photographer caused a year of frustrating delays that were overcome only after Carroll threatened legal action and obtained the rest of the plates. The Christmas week of 1886 was very much an 'Alice week': the facsimile was eventually published in an edition of 5,000 copies on Wednesday 22 December, the day before a theatrical version of *Alice* opened at the Prince of Wales' Theatre in London. Royalties from the facsimile went at Carroll's insistence to 'Children's Hospitals and Convalescent Homes for Sick Children'. The copy that Carroll gave to Alice was inscribed:

The enormous popularity of the Alice books was unabated by the passing of time, but as her granddaughter remarks, Alice herself gradually tired of her part in the business. In 1928, when Dodgson had been dead for 30 years and Alice was 75 years old, widowed and owing death duties, she decided to sell the manuscript. It was auctioned along with other Carroll books and memorabilia at Sotheby's in London on 3 April amid a storm of controversy as to whether it should be allowed to leave England. It fetched a staggering £15,400 (then equivalent to $77,000), a British auction record for any book, and naturally made front page news. It was acquired first by an American antiquarian bookdealer, A. S. W. Rosenbach of Philadelphia who in turn sold it for $150,000 to the multi-millionaire collector, Eldridge Reeves Johnson of Moorestown, New Jersey, founder of the Victor Talking Machine Company (the 'Victor' of the present-day RCA-Victor Corporation).

Alice herself visited the United States in 1932, at the age of 80 (she celebrated her eightieth birthday in New York) when she was invited to attend the events marking the centenary of the birth of Lewis Carroll. There she was fêted by the press and made a Doctor of Literature by Columbia University. She also met Eldridge Johnson, the new owner of *Alice's Adventures Under Ground* (who, incidentally, had a facsimile of his treasured manuscript privately printed in Vienna in the late 1930s).

Alice died in 1934 and after Johnson's death on 15 November 1945 the manuscript was again offered at auction. It appeared as Lot 51 in a sale at New York's Parke-Bernet Galleries on 3 April 1946. Luther H. Evans, Librarian of the Library of Congress, was concerned that it should be returned to its homeland and managed to raise funds among American bibliophiles in order to acquire it for the British people '. . . as the slightest token of recognition for the fact that they held off Hitler while we got ready for war'. The list of subscribers has never been made public, but is known to have included several distinguished people—including the manuscript's original purchaser, A. S. W. Rosenbach. Rival collectors held back in the bidding and it was bought by Evans for $50,000. After briefly displaying it in the New York Public Library, Evans travelled to England where he presented the volume to the manuscript department of the British Museum (now the British Library) on 13 November 1948. The Archbishop of Canterbury, Dr Geoffrey Fisher, accepting the manuscript on behalf of the Trustees of the British Museum and the British nation, described the gift as 'an unsullied and innocent act in a distracted and sinful world'. This generous and sincere gesture touched the sentiments of austere post-War Britain, and was reported alongside the other major news item of the day—the birth of Prince Charles.

The manuscript has remained on display in the British Museum ever since, returning once to America in 1982 for an exhibition at the Pierpont Morgan Library in New York to celebrate the 150th anniversary of Carroll's birth.

The story of *Alice's Adventures Under Ground* ends not quite here, but with a recent discovery. As previously mentioned, on the last page of the original manuscript, Carroll had stuck a portrait photograph of Alice, snipped into an oval from a portrait of his 'child-friend' taken by himself. He did not allow this to appear in the 1886 facsimile and it was not until a few years ago that the American Lewis Carroll expert, Morton N. Cohen, discovered that beneath the photograph lay Carroll's drawing of Alice. The two images have now been separated and both are reproduced in this new edition. The little vignette portrait sketch, his only known drawing of Alice, confirms what we already know from his photographs of her: that the long-haired Pre-Raphaelite-influenced Alice of Carroll's drawings and Tenniel's well-known illustrations, and the real-life Alice Liddell, with short hair cut in a fringe, are two different girls. They strangely symbolize the two Alices: the real Alice Liddell, sensitively drawn and photographed by Charles Dodgson, and 'Alice in Wonderland', the fantasy childhood heroine—created by the inventive genius of Lewis Carroll.

*'The Real Alice' by Carroll, 1859.*

## A Selective *Alice* Bibliography

Morton N. Cohen (ed.), *The Letters of Lewis Carroll*, London, Macmillan, 1979

Martin Gardner (ed.), *The Annotated Alice*, New York, Clarkson N. Potter, 1960; Harmondsworth, Penguin Books, 1965, revised edition 1970

Colin Gordon, *Beyond the Looking Glass*, London, Hodder & Stoughton, 1982

Roger Lancelyn Green (ed.), *The Diaries of Lewis Carroll*, London, Macmillan, 1953

Robert Phillips, *Aspects of Alice*, New York, Vanguard, 1971; London, Victor Gollancz, 1972; Harmondsworth, Penguin Books, 1974

A Christmas Gift
to
a Dear Child
in Memory
of
a Summer Day.

# Alice's Adventures under Ground

# Chapter 1

Alice was beginning to get very tired of sitting by her sister on the bank, and of having nothing to do: once or twice she had peeped into the book her sister was reading, but it had no pictures or conversations in it, and where is the use of a book, thought Alice, without pictures or conversations? So she was considering in her own mind, (as well as she could, for the hot day made her feel very sleepy and stupid,) whether the pleasure of making a daisy-chain was worth the trouble of getting up and picking the daisies, when a white rabbit with pink eyes ran close by her.

There was nothing very remarkable in that, nor did Alice think it so very much out of the way to hear the rabbit say to itself "dear, dear! I shall be too late!" (when she thought it over afterwards, it occurred to her that she ought to have wondered at this, but at the time it all seemed quite natural); but when the rabbit actually took a watch out of its waistcoat-pocket, looked at it, and then hurried on, Alice started to her feet, for it flashed across her mind that she had never before seen a rabbit with either a waistcoat-pocket or a watch to take out of it, and, full of curiosity, she hurried across the field after it, and was just in time to see it pop down a large rabbit-hole under the hedge. In a moment down went Alice after it, never once considering how in the world she was to get out again.

The rabbit-hole went straight on like a tunnel for some way, and then dipped suddenly down, so suddenly, that Alice had not a moment to think about stopping herself, before she found herself falling down what seemed a deep well. Either the well was very deep, or she fell very slowly, for she had plenty of time as she went down to look about her, and to wonder what would happen next. First, she tried to look down and make out what she was coming to, but it was too dark to see anything: then, she looked at the sides of the well, and noticed that they were filled with cupboards and book-shelves; here and there were maps and pictures hung on pegs. She took a jar down off one of of the shelves as she passed: it was labelled

"Orange Marmalade", but to her great disappoint--ment it was empty : she did not like to drop the jar, for fear of killing somebody underneath, so managed to put it into one of the cupboards as she fell past it.

"Well!" thought Alice to herself, "after such a fall as this, I shall think nothing of tumbling down stairs! How brave they'll all think me at home! Why, I wouldn't say anything about it, even if I fell off the top of the house!"(which was most likely true.)

Down, down, down. Would the fall never come to an end? "I wonder how many miles I've fallen by this time?" said she aloud, "I must be getting somewhere near the centre of the earth. Let me see: that would be four thousand miles down, I think —" (for you see Alice had learnt several things of this sort in her lessons in the schoolroom, and though this was not a very good opportunity of showing off her know--ledge, as there was no one to hear her, still it was good practice to say it over,) "yes, that's the right distance, but then what Longitude or Latitude-line shall I be in?" (Alice had no idea what Longitude was, or Latitude either, but she thought they were nice grand words to say.)

Presently she began again: "I wonder if I shall fall right <u>through</u> the earth! How funny it'll be to come out among the people that walk with their heads downwards! But I shall have to ask them what the name of the country is, you know. Please, Ma'am, is this New Zealand or Australia?"— and she tried to curtsey as she spoke, (fancy <u>curtseying</u> as you're falling through the air! do you think you could manage it?)"and what an ignorant little girl she'll think me for asking! No, it'll never do to ask: perhaps I shall see it written up somewhere."

Down, down, down: there was nothing else to do, so Alice soon began talking again. "Dinah will miss me very much tonight, I should think!" (Dinah was the cat.) "I hope they'll remember her saucer of milk at tea-time! Oh, dear Dinah, I wish I had you here! There are no mice in the air, I'm afraid, but you might catch a bat, and that's very like a mouse, you know, my dear. But do cats eat bats, I wonder?" And here Alice began to get rather sleepy, and kept on saying to herself, in a dreamy sort of way "do cats eat bats? do cats eat bats?" and sometimes, "do bats eat cats?" for, as she couldn't answer either question, it didn't much matter which way she put it. She felt that she was dozing off, and had just begun to dream that she was walking hand in hand with Dinah, and was saying to her very earnestly, "Now, Dinah, my dear, tell me the truth. Did you ever eat a bat?" when suddenly, bump! bump! down she came upon a heap of sticks and shavings, and the fall was over.

Alice was not a bit hurt, and jumped on to her feet directly: she looked up, but it was all dark overhead; before her was another long passage, and the white rabbit was still in sight, hurrying down it. There was not a moment to be lost: away went Alice like the wind, and just heard it say, as it turned a corner, "my ears and whiskers, how late it's getting!" She turned the corner after it, and instantly found herself in a long, low hall, lit up by a row of lamps which hung from the roof.

There were doors all round the hall, but they were all locked, and when Alice had been all round it, and tried them all, she walked sadly down the middle, wondering how she was ever to get out again: suddenly she came upon a little three-legged table, all made of solid glass; there was nothing lying upon it, but a tiny golden key, and Alice's first idea was that it might belong to one of the doors of the hall, but alas! either

the locks were too large, or the key too small, but at any rate it would open none of them. However, on the second time round, she came to a low curtain, behind which was a door about eighteen inches high: she tried the little key in the keyhole, and it fitted! Alice opened the door, and looked down a small passage, not larger than a rat-hole, into the loveliest garden you ever saw. How she longed to get out of that dark hall, and wander about among those beds of bright flowers and those cool fountains, but she could not even get her head through the doorway, "and even if my head would go through," thought poor Alice, "it would be very little use without my shoulders. Oh, how I wish I could shut up like a telescope! I think I could, if I only knew how to begin." For, you see, so many out--of-the-way things had happened lately, that Alice began to think very few things indeed were really impossible.

There was nothing else to do, so she went back to the table, half hoping she might find another key on it, or at any rate a book of rules for shutting up people like telescopes : this time there was a little bottle on it—" which certainly was not there before" said Alice — and tied round the neck of the bottle was a paper label with the words DRINK ME beautifully printed on it in large letters.

It was all very well. to say "drink me", "but I'll look first," said the wise little Alice, "and see whether the bottle's marked "poison" or not," for Alice had read several nice little stories about children that got burnt, and eaten up by wild beasts, and other unpleasant things, because they would not remember the simple rules their friends had given them, such as, that , if you get into the fire, it will burn you, and that, if you cut your finger very deeply with a knife, it generally bleeds, and she had never forgotten that, if you drink a bottle marked "poison", it is almost certain to disagree with you, sooner or later.

However, this bottle was _not_ marked poison, so Alice tasted it, and finding it very nice, ( it had, in fact, a sort of mixed flavour of cherry-tart, custard, pine-apple, roast turkey, toffy, and hot buttered toast,) she very soon finished it off.

*　　*　　*　　*　　*　　*

"What a curious feeling!" said Alice, "I must be shutting up like a telescope."

It was so indeed: she was now only ten inches high, and her face brightened up as it occurred to her that she was now the right size for going through the little door into that lovely garden. First, however, she waited for a few minutes to see whether she was going to shrink any further: she felt a little nervous about this, "for it might end, you know," said Alice to herself, "in my going out altogether, like a candle, and what should I be like then, I wonder?" and she tried to fancy what the flame of a candle is like after the candle is blown out,

for she could not remember having ever
seen one. However, nothing more happened,
so she decided on going into the garden
at once, but, alas for poor Alice! when she
got to the door, she found she had forgotten
the little golden key, and when she went back
to the table for the key, she found she
could not possibly reach it: she could
see it plainly enough through the glass,
and she tried her best to climb up one of
the legs of the table, but it was too slippery,
and when she had tired herself out with
trying, the poor little thing sat down and cried.

"Come! there's
no use in crying!"
said Alice to herself
rather sharply, "I
advise you to leave
off this minute!"(she
generally gave herself
very good advice, and
sometimes scolded

herself so severely as to bring tears into her
eyes, and once she remembered boxing her
own ears for having been unkind to herself

in a game of croquet she was playing with herself, for this curious child was very fond of pretending to be two people,) "but it's no use now", thought poor Alice, "to pretend to be two people! Why, there's hardly enough of me left to make one respectable person!"

Soon her eyes fell on a little ebony box lying under the table: she opened it, and found in it a very small cake, on which was lying a card with the words EAT ME beautifully printed on it in large letters. "I'll eat," said Alice, "and if it makes me larger, I can reach the key, and if it makes me smaller, I can creep under the door, so either way I'll get into the garden, and I don't care which happens!"

She eat a little bit, and said anxiously to herself "which way? which way?" and laid her hand on the top of her head to feel which way it was growing, and was quite surprised to find that she remained the same size: to be sure this is what generally happens when one eats cake, but Alice had got into the way of expecting nothing but out-
-of-the way things to happen, and it seemed

quite dull and stupid for things to
go on in the common way.

So she set to work, and very
soon finished off the cake.

\*    \*    \*    \*    \*

"Curiouser and curiouser!" cried
Alice, (she was so surprised, that she
quite forgot how to speak good English,)
"now I'm opening out like the largest
telescope that ever was! Goodbye,
feet!" (for when she looked down
at her feet, they seemed almost
out of sight, they were getting so
far off,) "oh, my poor little feet, I
wonder who will put on your shoes
and stockings for you now, dears?
I'm sure I ca'n't! I shall be a great
deal too far off to bother myself about
you : you must manage the best
way you can — but I must be kind
to them", thought Alice, "or perhaps
they won't walk the way I want
to go! Let me see : I'll give them
a new pair of boots every Christmas."

And she went on planning
to herself how she would manage it:

"they must go by the carrier," she thought,
"and how funny it'll seem, sending presents
to one's own feet! And how odd the directions
will look! ALICE'S RIGHT FOOT, ESQ.
           THE CARPET,
               with ALICE'S LOVE.
oh dear! what nonsense I am talking!"

Just at this moment, her head struck
against the roof of the hall: in fact, she
was now rather more than nine feet high,
and she at once took up the little golden
key, and hurried off to the garden door.

Poor Alice! it was as much as she
could do, lying down on one side, to look
through into the garden with one eye, but
to get through was more hopeless than ever:
she sat down and cried again.

"You ought to be ashamed of yourself,"
said Alice, "a great girl like you," (she might
well say this,) "to cry in this way! Stop this
instant, I tell you!" But she cried on all
the same, shedding gallons of tears, until
there was a large pool, about four inches
deep, all round her, and reaching half way
across the hall. After a time, she heard a
little pattering of feet in the distance, and

dried her eyes to see what was coming. It was the white rabbit coming back again, splendidly dressed, with a pair of white kid gloves in one hand, and a nosegay in the other. Alice was ready to ask help of any one, she felt so desperate, and as the rabbit passed her, she said, in a low, timid voice, "If you please, Sir——" the rabbit started violently, looked up once into the roof of the hall, from which the voice seemed to come, and then dropped the nosegay and the white kid gloves, and skurried away into the dark--ness as hard as it could go.

Alice took up the nosegay and gloves, and found the nosegay so delicious that she kept smelling at it all the time she went on talking to herself—— "dear, dear! how queer everything is today! and yester--day everything happened just as usual: I wonder if I was changed in the night? Let me think: was I the same when I got up this morning? I think I remember feeling rather different. But if I'm not the same, who in the world am I? Ah, that's the great puzzle!" And she began thinking over all the children she knew of the same age as herself, to see if she could have been changed for any of them.

"I'm sure I'm not Gertrude," she said, "for her hair goes in such long ringlets, and mine doesn't go in ringlets at all — and I'm sure I can't be Florence, for I know all sorts of things, and she, oh! she knows such a very little! Besides, she's she, and I'm I, and — oh dear! how puzzling it all is! I'll try if I know all the things I used to know. Let me see: four times five is twelve, and four times six is thirteen, and four times seven is fourteen — oh dear! I shall never get to twenty at this rate! But the Multiplication Table don't signify — let's try Geography. London is the capital of France, and Rome is the capital of Yorkshire, and Paris — oh dear! dear! that's all wrong, I'm certain! I must have been changed for Florence! I'll try and say "How doth the little"," and she crossed her hands on her lap, and began, but her voice sounded hoarse and strange, and the words did not sound the same as they used to do:

"How doth the little crocodile
   Improve its shining tail,
And pour the waters of the Nile
   On every golden scale!

How cheerfully it seems to grin!
   How neatly spreads its claws!
And welcomes little fishes in
   With gently-smiling jaws!"

"I'm sure those are not the right words," said poor Alice, and her eyes filled with tears as she thought "I must be Florence after all, and I shall have to go and live in that poky little house, and have next to no toys to play with, and oh! ever so many lessons to learn! No! I've made up my mind about it: if I'm Florence, I'll stay down here! It'll be no use their putting their heads down and saying 'come up, dear!' I shall only look up and say 'who am I, then? answer me that first, and then, if I like being that person, I'll come up: if not, I'll stay down here till I'm somebody else —— but, oh dear!" cried Alice with a sudden burst of tears, "I do wish they <u>would</u> put their heads down! I am so tired of being all alone here!"

As she said this, she looked down at her hands, and was surprised to find she had put on one of the rabbit's little gloves while she was talking. "How <u>can</u> I have done that?" thought she, "I must be growing small again." She got up and went to the table to measure herself by it, and found that, as nearly as she could guess, she was now about two feet high, and was going on shrinking rapidly: soon she found out that the reason of it was the nosegay she held in her hand: she dropped it hastily, just in time to save herself from shrinking away altogether, and found that she was now only three inches high.

"Now for the garden!" cried Alice,

as she hurried back to the little door,
but the little door was locked again, and
the little gold key was lying on the glass
table as before, and "things are worse
than ever!" thought the poor little girl,
"for I never was as small as this before,
never! And I declare it's too bad, it is!"

At this moment
her foot slipped,
and splash! she
was up to her chin
in salt water. Her
first idea was
that she had
fallen into the
sea : then she
remembered that
she was under
ground, and she
soon made out that it was the pool of tears she
had wept when she was nine feet high. "I wish
I hadn't cried so much!" said Alice, as she
swam about, trying to find her way out, "I
shall be punished for it now, I suppose, by
being drowned in my own tears! Well! that'll

be a queer thing, to be sure! However, every thing is queer today." Very soon she saw something splashing about in the pool near her: at first she thought it must be a walrus or a hippopotamus, but then she remembered how small she was herself, and soon made out that it was only a mouse, that had slipped in like herself.

"Would it be any use, now," thought Alice, "to speak to this mouse? The rabbit is something quite out-of-the-way, no doubt, and so have I been, ever since I came down here, but that is no reason why the mouse should not be able to talk. I think I may as well try."

So she began: "oh Mouse, do you know how to get out of this pool? I am very tired of swimming about here, oh Mouse!" The mouse looked at her rather inquisitively, and seemed to her to wink with one of its little eyes, but it said nothing.

"Perhaps it doesn't understand English," thought Alice; "I daresay it's a French mouse, come over with William the Conqueror!" (for,

with all her knowledge of history, Alice had no very clear notion how long ago anything had happened,) so she began again: "où est "ma chatte?" which was the first sentence out of her French lesson-book. The mouse gave a sudden jump in the pool, and seemed to quiver with fright: "oh, I beg your pardon!" cried Alice hastily, afraid that she had hurt the poor animal's feelings, "I quite forgot "you didn't like cats!"

"Not like cats!" cried the mouse, in a shrill, passionate voice, "would you like cats if you were me?"

"Well, perhaps not," said Alice in a soothing tone, "don't be angry about it. "And yet I wish I could show you our cat Dinah: I think you'd take a fancy to cats if you could only see her. She is such a dear quiet thing," said Alice, half to herself, as she swam lazily about in the pool, "she sits purring so nicely by the fire, licking her paws and washing her face: and she is such a nice soft thing to nurse, and she's such a capital one for catching mice — oh! I beg your pardon!" cried poor Alice again, for this time the mouse was bristling all over, and she felt certain that it was really offended, "have I offended you?"

"Offended indeed!" cried the mouse, who seemed to be positively trembling with rage, "our family always _hated_ cats! Nasty, low, vulgar things! Don't talk to me about them any more!"

"I won't indeed!" said Alice, in a great hurry to change the conversation, "are you— "are you — fond of — dogs?" The mouse did not answer, so Alice went on eagerly: "there is such a nice little dog near our house I should like to show you! A little bright- -eyed terrier, you know, with oh! such long curly brown hair! And it'll fetch things when you throw them, and it'll sit up and beg for its dinner, and all sorts of things — I can't remember half of them — and it belongs to a farmer, and he says it kills all the rats and — oh dear!" said Alice sadly, "I'm afraid I've offended it again!" for the mouse was swimming away from her as hard as it could go, and making quite a commotion in the pool as it went.

So she called softly after it: "mouse dear! Do come back again, and we won't talk about cats and dogs any more, if you don't like them!" When the mouse heard this, it turned and swam slowly back to her: its face was quite pale, (with passion, Alice thought,) and it said in a trembling low voice "let's get to the shore, and then I'll tell you my history, and you'll understand why it is I hate cats and dogs."

It was high time to go, for the pool was getting quite full of birds and animals that had fallen into it. There was a Duck and a Dodo, a Lory and an Eaglet, and several other curious creatures. Alice led the way, and the whole party swam to the shore.

# Chapter 11

They were indeed a curious looking party that assembled on the bank — the birds with draggled feathers, the animals with their fur clinging close to them — all dripping wet, cross, and uncomfortable. The first question of course was, how to get dry: they had a consultation about this, and Alice hardly felt at all surprised at finding her-self talking familiarly with the birds, as if she had known them all her life. Indeed, she had quite a long argument with the Lory, who at last turned sulky, and would only say "I am older than you, and must know best", and this Alice would not admit without knowing how old the Lory was, and as the Lory positively refused to tell its age, there was nothing more to be said.

At last the mouse, who seemed to have some authority among them, called out "sit down, all of you, and attend to me! I'll soon make you dry enough!" They all sat down at once, shivering, in a large ring, Alice in the middle, with her eyes anxiously fixed on the mouse, for she felt sure she would catch a bad cold if she did not get dry very soon.

"Ahem!" said the mouse, with a self-important air, "are you all ready? This is the driest thing I know. Silence all round, if you please!

"William the Conqueror, whose cause was favoured by the pope, was soon submitted to by the English, who wanted leaders, and had been of late much accustomed to usurpation and conquest. Edwin and Morcar, the earls of Mercia and Northumbria ——"

"Ugh!" said the Lory with a shiver.

"I beg your pardon?" said the mouse, frowning, but very politely, "did you speak?"

"Not I!" said the Lory hastily.

"I thought you did," said the mouse, "I proceed. Edwin and Morcar, the earls of Mercia and Northumbria, declared for him;

and even Stigand, the patriotic archbishop of Canterbury, found it advisable to go with Edgar Atheling to meet William and offer him the crown. William's conduct was at first moderate — how are you getting on now, dear?" said the mouse, turning to Alice as it spoke.

"As wet as ever," said poor Alice," it doesn't seem to dry me at all."

"In that case," said the Dodo solemnly, rising to his feet," I move that the meeting adjourn, for the immediate adoption of more energetic remedies ——"

"Speak English!" said the Duck," I don't know the meaning of half those long words, and what's more, I don't believe you do either!" And the Duck quacked a com-fortable laugh to itself. Some of the other birds tittered audibly.

"I only meant to say," said the Dodo in a rather offended tone," that I know of a house near here, where we could get the young lady and the rest of the party dried, and then we could listen comfortably to the story which I think you were good enough to promise to tell us," bowing gravely to the mouse.

The mouse made no objection to this, and the whole party moved along the river bank, ( for the pool had by this time begun to flow out of the hall, and the edge of it was fringed with rushes and forget-me-nots,) in a slow procession, the Dodo leading the way. After a time the Dodo became impatient, and, leaving the Duck to bring up the rest of the party, moved on at a quicker pace with Alice, the Lory, and the Eaglet, and soon brought them to a little cottage, and there they sat snugly by the fire, wrapped up in blankets, until the rest of the party had arrived, and they were all dry again.

Then they all sat down again in a large ring on the bank, and begged the mouse to begin his story.

"Mine is a long and a sad tale!" said the mouse, turning to Alice, and sighing.

"It is a long tail, certainly," said Alice, looking down with wonder at the mouse's tail, which was coiled nearly all round the party, "but why do you call it sad?" and she went on puzzling about this as the mouse went on speaking, so that her idea of the tale was something like this:

We lived beneath the mat
    Warm and snug and fat
        But one woe, & that
            Was the cat!
                To our joys
                a clog, In
                our eyes a
                fog, On our
            hearts a log
        Was the dog!
    When the
cat's away,
Then
the mice
will
play,
    But, alas!
        one day, (So they say)
            Came the dog and
                cat, Hunting
                    for a
                    rat,
                    Crushed
                the mice
            all flat,
            Each
            one
            as
            he
            sat
            Underneath the mat, Warm & snug & fat – Think of that!

"You are not attending!" said the mouse to Alice severely, "what are you thinking of?"

"I beg your pardon," said Alice very humbly, "you had got to the fifth bend, I think?"

"I had _not_!" cried the mouse, sharply and very angrily.

"A knot!" said Alice, always ready to make herself useful, and looking anxiously about her, "oh, do let me help to undo it!"

"I shall do nothing of the sort!" said the mouse, getting up and walking away from the party, "you insult me by talking such nonsense!".

"I didn't mean it!" pleaded poor Alice, "but you're so easily offended, you know."

The mouse only growled in reply.

"Please come back and finish your story!" Alice called after it, and the others all joined in chorus "yes, please do!" but the mouse only shook its ears, and walked quickly away, and was soon out of sight.

"What a pity it wouldn't stay!" sighed the Lory, and an old Crab took the oppor- tunity of saying to its daughter "Ah, my dear!

let this be a lesson to you never to lose your temper!" "Hold your tongue, Ma!" said the young Crab, a little snappishly, "you're enough to try the patience of an oyster!"

"I wish I had our Dinah here, I know I do!" said Alice aloud, addressing no one in particular, "she'd soon fetch it back!"

"And who is Dinah, if I might venture to ask the question?" said the Lory.

Alice replied eagerly, for she was always ready to talk about her pet, "Dinah's our cat. And she's such a capital one for catching mice, you can't think! And oh! I wish you could see her after the birds! Why, she'll eat a little bird as soon as look at it!"

This answer caused a remarkable sensation among the party; some of the birds hurried off at once; one old magpie began wrapping itself up very carefully, remarking "I really must be getting home: the night air does not suit my throat," and a canary called out in a trembling voice to its children "come away from her, my dears, she's no fit company for you!" On various pretexts, they all moved off, and Alice was soon left alone.

She sat for some while sorrowful and silent, but she was not long before she recovered her spirits, and began talking to herself again as usual: "I do wish some of them had stayed a little longer! and I was getting to be such friends with them — really the Lory and I were almost like sisters! and so was that dear little Eaglet! And then the Duck and the Dodo! How nicely the Duck sang to us as we came along through the water: and if the Dodo hadn't known the way to that nice little cottage, I don't know when we should have got dry again ——" and there is no knowing how long she might have prattled on in this way, if she had not suddenly caught the sound of pattering feet.

It was the white rabbit, trotting slowly back again, and looking anxiously about it as it went, as if it had lost something, and she heard it muttering to itself "the Marchioness! the Marchioness! oh my dear paws! oh my fur and whiskers! She'll have me executed, as sure as ferrets

are ferrets! Where _can_ I have dropped them,
I wonder?" Alice guessed in a moment that
it was looking for the nosegay and the pair
of white kid gloves, and she began hunting
for them, but they were now nowhere to be
seen — everything seemed to have changed
since her swim in the pool, and her walk
along the river—bank with its fringe of
rushes and forget-me-nots, and the glass
table and the little door had vanished.

Soon the rabbit
noticed Alice, as
she stood looking
curiously about
her, and at once
said in a quick
angry tone, "why,
Mary Ann! what
_are_ you doing out
here? Go home this
moment, and look
on my dressing-table for my gloves and nosegay,
and fetch them here, as quick as you can
run, do you hear?" and Alice was so much
frightened that she ran off at once, without

saying a word, in the direction which the rabbit had pointed out

She soon found herself in front of a neat little house, on the door of which was a bright brass plate with the name W. RABBIT, ESQ. she went in, and hurried upstairs, for fear she should meet the real Mary Ann and be turned out of the house before she had found the gloves: she knew that one pair had been lost in the hall, "but of course", thought Alice, "it has plenty more of them in its house. How queer it seems to be going messages for a rabbit! I suppose Dinah'll be sending me messages next!" And she began fancying the sort of things that would happen: "Miss Alice! come here directly and get ready for your walk!" "Coming in a minute, nurse! but I've got to watch this mousehole till Dinah comes back, and see that the mouse doesn't get out ——" "only I don't think," Alice went on, "that they'd let Dinah stop in the house, if it began ordering people about like that!"

By this time she had found her way into a tidy little room, with a table in the window on which was a looking-glass and, (as Alice had hoped,) two or three pairs of tiny white kid gloves: she took up a pair of gloves, and was just going to leave the room, when her eye fell upon a little bottle that stood near the looking-glass: there was no label on it this time with the words "drink me", but nevertheless she uncorked it and put it

to her lips: "I know something interesting is sure to happen," she said to herself, "whenever I eat or drink anything, so I'll see what this bottle does. I do hope it'll make me grow larger, for I'm quite tired of being such a tiny little thing!"

It did so indeed, and much sooner

than she expected; before she had drunk half the bottle, she found her head pressing against the ceiling, and she stooped to save her neck from being broken, and hastily put down the bottle, saying to herself "that's quite enough— I hope I sha'n't grow any more— I wish I hadn't drunk so much!"

Alas! it was too late: she went on growing and growing, and very soon had to kneel down: in another minute there was not room even for this, and she tried the effect of lying down, with one elbow against the door, and the other arm curled round her head. Still she went on growing, and as a last resource she put one arm out of the window, and one foot up the chimney, and said to herself "now I can do no more — what will become of me?"

Luckily for Alice, the little magic bottle had now had its full effect, and she grew no larger: still it was very uncomfortable, and as there seemed to be no sort of chance of ever getting out of the room again, no wonder she felt unhappy. "It was much pleasanter at home," thought poor Alice, "when one wasn't always growing larger and smaller, and being ordered about by mice and rabbits — I almost wish I hadn't gone down that rabbit-hole, and yet, and yet — it's rather curious, you know, this sort of life. I do wonder what <u>can</u> have happened to me! When I used to read fairy-tales, I fancied that sort of thing never happened, and now here I am in the middle of one! There ought to be a book written about me, that there ought! and when I grow up I'll write one — but I'm grown up now" said she in a sorrowful tone, "at least there's no room to grow up any more <u>here</u>."

"But then", thought Alice, "shall I <u>never</u> get any older than I am now? That'll be a comfort, one way — never to be an old woman — but then — always to have lessons to learn! Oh, I shouldn't like _that_!"

"Oh, you foolish Alice!" she said again, "how can you learn lessons in here? Why, there's hardly room for you, and no room at all for any lesson-books!"

And so she went on, taking first one side, and then the other, and making quite a conversation of it altogether, but after a few minutes she heard a voice outside, which made her stop to listen.

"Mary Ann! Mary Ann!" said the voice, "fetch me my gloves this moment!" Then came a little pattering of feet on the stairs: Alice knew it was the rabbit coming to look for her, and she trembled till she shook the house, quite forgetting that she was now about a thousand times as large as the rabbit, and had no reason to be afraid of it. Presently the rabbit came to the door, and tried to open it, but as it opened inwards, and Alice's elbow was against it, the attempt proved a failure. Alice heard it say to itself "then I'll go round and get in at the window."

"That you won't!" thought Alice, and, after waiting till she fancied she heard the rabbit just under the window, she suddenly spread out her hand, and made a snatch in the air. She did not get hold of anything, but she heard a little shriek and a fall and a crash of breaking glass, from which she concluded that it was just possible it had fallen into a cucumber-frame, or something of the sort.

Next came an angry voice — the rabbit's — "Pat, Pat! where are you?" And then a voice she had never heard before, "shure then I'm here! digging for apples, anyway, yer honour!"

"Digging for apples indeed!" said the rabbit angrily, "here, come and help me.

out of _this_!" — Sound of more breaking glass.

"Now, tell me, Pat, what is that coming out of the window?"

"Shure it's an arm, yer honour!" (He pronounced it "arrum".)

"An arm, you goose! Who ever saw an arm that size? Why, it fills the whole window, don't you see?"

"Shure, it does, yer honour, but it's an arm for all that."

"Well, it's no business there: go and take it away!"

There was a long silence after this, and Alice could only hear whispers now and then, such as "shure I don't like it, yer honour, at all at all!" "do as I tell you, you coward!" and at last she spread out her hand again and made another snatch in the air. This time there were _two_ little shrieks, and more breaking glass — "what a number of cucumber-frames there must be!" thought Alice, "I wonder what they'll do next! As for pulling me out of the window, I only wish they _could_! I'm sure _I_ don't want to stop in here any longer!"

She waited for some time without

hearing anything more : at last came a rumbling of little cart-wheels, and the sound of a good many voices all talking together : she made out the words "where's the other ladder? — why, I hadn't to bring but one, Bill's got the other — here, put 'em up at this corner — no, tie 'em together first — they don't reach high enough yet — oh, they'll do well enough, don't be particular — here, Bill! catch hold of this rope — will the roof bear? — mind that loose slate — oh, it's coming down! heads below! —" (a loud crash) "now, who did that? — it was Bill, I fancy — who's to go down the chimney? — nay, I shan't! you do it! — that I won't then — Bill's got to go down — here, Bill! the master says you've to go down the chimney!"

"Oh, so Bill's got to come down the chimney, has he?" said Alice to herself, "why, they seem to put everything upon Bill! I wouldn't be in Bill's place for a good deal : the fireplace is a pretty tight one, but I think I can kick a little!"

She drew her foot as far down the chimney as she could, and waited till she heard a little animal (she couldn't guess what sort it was) scratching and scrambling in the chimney close above her: then, saying to herself "this is Bill", she gave

one sharp kick, and waited again to see what would happen next.

The first thing was a general chorus of "there goes Bill!" then the rabbit's voice alone "catch him, you by the hedge!" then silence, and then another confusion of voices, "how was it, old fellow? what happened to you? tell us all about it."

Last came a little feeble squeaking voice, ("that's Bill" thought Alice,) which said "well, I hardly know — I'm all of a fluster myself — something comes at me like a Jack-in-the-box, and the next minute up I goes like a rocket!" "And so you did, old fellow!" said the other voices.

"We must burn the house down!" said the voice of the rabbit, and Alice called out as loud as she could "if you do, I'll set Dinah at you!" This caused silence again, and while Alice was thinking "but how can I get Dinah here?" she found to her great delight that she was getting smaller: very soon she was able to get up out of the uncomfortable position in which she had been lying, and in two or three minutes more she was once more three inches high.

She ran out of the house as quick as she could, and found quite a crowd of little animals waiting outside — guinea-pigs, white mice, squirrels, and "Bill" a little green lizard, that was being supported in the arms of one of the guinea-pigs, while another was giving it something out of a bottle. They all made a rush at her the moment she up-peared, but Alice ran her hardest, and soon found herself in a thick wood.

# Chapter III.

"The first thing
I've got to do," said
Alice to herself, as
she wandered about
in the wood, "is to
grow to my right
size, and the second
thing is to find my
way into that lovely
garden. I think that
will be the best plan".

It sounded an excellent plan, no doubt,
and very neatly and simply arranged : the only
difficulty was, that she had not the smallest
idea how to set about it, and while she was
peering anxiously among the trees round her,
a little sharp bark just over her head made
her look up in a great hurry.

An enormous puppy was looking down
at her with large round eyes, and feebly
stretching out one paw, trying to reach her :
"poor thing !" said Alice in a coaxing tone,

and she tried hard to whistle to it, but she was terribly alarmed all the while at the thought that it might be hungry, in which case it would probably devour her in spite of all her coaxing. Hardly knowing what she did, she picked up a little bit of stick, and held it out to the puppy: whereupon the puppy jumped into the air off all its feet at once, and with a yelp of delight rushed at the stick, and made believe to worry it: then Alice dodged behind a great thistle to keep herself from being run over, and, the moment she appeared at the other side, the puppy made another dart at the stick, and tumbled head over heels in its hurry to get hold: then Alice, thinking it was very like having a game of play with a cart-horse, and expecting every moment to be trampled under its feet, ran round the thistle again: then the puppy began a series of short charges at the stick, running a very little way forwards each time and a long way back, and barking hoarsely all the while, till at last it sat down a good way off, panting, with its tongue hanging out of its mouth, and its great eyes half shut.

This seemed to Alice a good opportunity for making her escape: she set off at once, and ran till the puppy's bark sounded quite faint in the distance, and till she was quite tired and out of breath.

"And yet what a dear little puppy it was!" said Alice, as she leant against a buttercup to rest herself, and fanned herself with her hat, "I should have liked teaching it tricks, if — if I'd only been the right size to do it! Oh! I'd nearly forgotten that I've got to grow up again! Let me see: how is it to be managed? I suppose I ought to eat or drink something or other, but the great question is, what?"

The great question certainly was, what? Alice looked all round her at the flowers and the blades of grass, but could not see anything that looked like the right thing to eat under the circumstances. There was a large mushroom near her, about the same height as herself, and when she had looked under it, and on both sides of it, and behind it, it occurred to her to look and see what was on the top of it.

She stretched herself up on tiptoe, and peeped over the edge of the mushroom,

and her eyes immediately met those of a large blue caterpillar, which was sitting with its arms fold-ed, quietly smoking a long hookah, and taking not the least notice of her or of anything else.

For some time they looked at each other in silence: at last the caterpillar took the hookah out of its mouth, and languidly addressed her.

"Who are you?" said the caterpillar.

This was not an encouraging opening for a conversation: Alice replied rather shyly, "I — I hardly know, sir, just at present— at least I know who I <u>was</u> when I got up this morning, but I think I must have been changed several times since that."

"What do you mean by that?" said the caterpillar, "explain yourself!"

"I ca'nt explain <u>myself</u>, I'm afraid, sir,"

said Alice, "because I'm not myself, you see."

"I don't see," said the caterpillar.

"I'm afraid I can't put it more clearly," Alice replied very politely, "for I can't under-stand it myself, and really to be so many different sizes in one day is very confusing."

"It isn't," said the caterpillar.

"Well, perhaps you haven't found it so yet," said Alice, "but when you have to turn into a chrysalis, you know, and then after that into a butterfly, I should think it'll feel a little queer, don't you think so?"

"Not a bit," said the caterpillar.

"All I know is," said Alice, "it would feel queer to _me_."

"_You_!" said the caterpillar contemptu-ously, "who are you?"

Which brought them back again to the beginning of the conversation: Alice felt a little irritated at the caterpillar making such very short remarks, and she drew her-self up and said very gravely "I think you ought to tell me who _you_ are, first."

"Why?" said the caterpillar.

Here was another puzzling question:

and as Alice had no reason ready, and the caterpillar seemed to be in a very bad temper, she turned round and walked away.

"Come back!" the caterpillar called after her, "I've something important to say!"

This sounded promising: Alice turned and came back again.

"Keep your temper," said the caterpillar.

"Is that all?" said Alice, swallowing down her anger as well as she could.

"No," said the caterpillar.

Alice thought she might as well wait, as she had nothing else to do, and perhaps after all the caterpillar might tell her something worth hearing. For some minutes it puffed away at its hookah without speaking, but at last it unfolded its arms, took the hookah out of its mouth again, and said "so you think you're changed, do you?"

"Yes, sir," said Alice, "I can't remember the things I used to know — I've tried to say "How doth the little busy bee" and it came all different!"

"Try and repeat "You are old, father William"," said the caterpillar.

Alice folded her hands, and began:

1

"You are old, father William," the young man said,
   "And your hair is exceedingly white :
And yet you incessantly stand on your head —
   Do you think, at your age, it is right ?"

2.

"In my youth," father William replied to his son,
   "I feared it might injure the brain :
But now that I'm perfectly sure I have none,
   Why, I do it again and again."

"You are old," said the youth, "as I mentioned before,
  "And have grown most uncommonly fat:
Yet you turned a back-somersault in at the door —
  Pray what is the reason of that?"

4.

"In my youth," said the sage, as he shook his gray locks,
  "I kept all my limbs very supple.
By the use of this ointment, five shillings. the box —
  Allow me to sell you a couple."

5.

"You are old," said the youth, "and your jaws are too weak
"For anything tougher than suet :
Yet you eat all the goose, with the bones and the beak —
Pray, how did you manage to do it ?"

6.

"In my youth," said the old man, "I took to the law,
And argued each case with my wife,
And the muscular strength, which it gave to my jaw,
Has lasted the rest of my life."

7.

"You are old", said the youth, "one would hardly suppose
    "That your eye was as steady as ever:
Yet you balanced an eel on the end of your nose——
    What made you so awfully clever ?"

8.

"I have answered three questions, and that is enough,"
    Said his father, "don't give yourself airs!
"Do you think I can listen all day to such stuff ?
    Be off, or I'll kick you down stairs !"

"That is not said right," said the caterpillar.

"Not quite right, I'm afraid," said Alice timidly, "some of the words have got altered."

"It is wrong from beginning to end," said the caterpillar decidedly, and there was silence for some minutes: the caterpillar was the first to speak.

"What size do you want to be?" it asked.

"Oh, I'm not particular as to size," Alice hastily replied, "only one doesn't like changing so often, you know."

"Are you content now?" said the caterpillar.

"Well, I should like to be a little larger, sir, if you wouldn't mind," said Alice, "three inches is such a wretched height to be."

"It is a very good height indeed!" said the caterpillar loudly and angrily, rearing itself straight up as it spoke (it was exactly three inches high).

"But I'm not used to it!" pleaded poor Alice in a piteous tone, and she thought to herself "I wish the creatures wouldn't be so easily offended!"

"You'll get used to it in time", said the caterpillar, and it put the hookah into its mouth, and began smoking again.

This time Alice waited quietly until it chose to speak again: in a few minutes the caterpillar took the hookah out of its mouth, and got down off the mushroom, and crawled away into the grass, merely remarking as it went: "the top will make you grow taller, and the stalk will make you grow shorter."

"The top of _what_? the stalk of _what_?" thought Alice.

"Of the mushroom," said the caterpillar, just as if she had asked it aloud, and in another moment it was out of sight.

Alice remained looking thoughtfully at the mushroom for a minute, and then picked it and carefully broke it in two,

taking the stalk in one hand, and the top in the other. "_Which_ does the stalk do?" she said, and nibbled a little bit of it to try: the next moment she felt a violent blow on her chin: it had struck her foot!

She was a good deal frightened by this very sudden change, but as she did not shrink any further, and had not dropped the top of the mushroom, she did not give up hope yet. There was hardly room to open her mouth, with her chin pressing against her foot, but she did it at last, and managed to bite off a little bit of the top of the mushroom.

\* \* \* \* \*

"Come! my head's free at last!" said Alice in a tone of delight, which changed into alarm in another mo-ment, when she found that her shoulders were nowhere to be seen: she looked down upon an immense length of neck, which seemed to rise like a stalk out of a sea of green leaves that lay far below her.

"What can all that green stuff be?" said Alice, "and where have my shoulders got to? And oh! my poor hands! how is it I can't see you?" She was moving them about as she spoke, but no result seemed to follow, except a little rustling among the leaves. Then she tried to bring her head down to her hands, and was delighted to find that her neck would bend about easily in every direction, like a serpent. She had just succeeded in bending it down in a beautiful zig-zag, and was going to dive in among the leaves, which she found to be the tops of the trees of the wood she had been wandering in, when a sharp hiss made her draw back: a large pigeon had flown into her face, and was vio- -lently beating her with its wings. "Serpent!" screamed the pigeon. "I'm not a serpent!" said Alice indignantly, "let me alone!"

"I've tried every way!" the pigeon said desperately, with a kind of sob: " nothing seems to suit 'em!"

"I haven't the least idea what you mean," said Alice.

"I've tried the roots of trees, and I've tried banks, and I've tried hedges," the pigeon went on without attending to her, "but them serpents! There's no pleasing 'em!"

Alice was more and more puzzled, but she thought there was no use in saying anything till the pigeon had finished.

"As if it wasn't trouble enough hatching the eggs!" said the pigeon, "without being on the look out for serpents, day and night! Why, I haven't had a wink of sleep these three weeks!"

"I'm very sorry you've been annoyed," said Alice, beginning to see its meaning.

"And just as I'd taken the highest tree in the wood," said the pigeon raising its voice to a shriek, "and was just thinking I was free of 'em at last, they must needs come down from the sky! Ugh! Serpent!"

"But I'm not a serpent," said Alice, "I'm a — I'm a — "

"Well! What are you?" said the pigeon, "I see you're trying to invent something."

"I— I'm a little girl," said Alice, rather doubtfully, as she remembered the number of changes she had gone through.

"A likely story indeed!" said the pigeon, "I've seen a good many of them in my time, but never one with such a neck as yours! No, you're a serpent, I know that well enough! I suppose you'll tell me next that you never tasted an egg!"

"I have tasted eggs, certainly," said Alice, who was a very truthful child, "but indeed I don't want any of yours. I don't like them raw."

"Well, be off, then!" said the pigeon, and settled down into its nest again. Alice crouched down among the trees, as well as she could, as her neck kept getting entangled among the branches, and several times she had to stop and untwist it. Soon she re--membered the pieces of mushroom which she still held in her hands, and set to work very carefully, nibbling first at one and then at the other, and growing sometimes taller and sometimes shorter, until she had suc--ceeded in bringing herself down to her usual size.

It was so long since she had been of the right size that it felt quite strange at first, but she got quite used to it in a minute or two, and began talking to herself as usual : "well! there's half my plan done now! How puzzling all these changes are! I'm never sure what I'm going to be, from one minute to another! However, I've got to my right size again : the next thing is, to get into that beautiful garden — how is that to be done, I wonder?"

Just as she said this, she noticed that one of the trees had a doorway leading right into it. "That's very curious!" she thought, "but everything's curious today : I may as well go in." And in she went.

Once more she found herself in the long hall, and close to the little glass table: "now, I'll manage better this time" she said to herself, and began by taking the little golden key, and unlocking the door that led into the garden. Then she set to work eating the pieces of mushroom till she was about fifteen inches high : then she walked down the little passage : and then — she found herself at last in the beautiful garden, among the bright flowerbeds and the cool fountains.

# Chapter IV

A large rose tree stood near the entrance of the garden : the roses on it were white, but there were three gardeners at it, busily painting them red . This Alice thought a very curious thing, and she went near to watch them , and just as she came up she heard one of them say " look out, Five ! Don't go splashing paint over me like that !"

"I couldn't help it," said Five in a sulky tone, " Seven jogged my elbow."

On which Seven lifted up his head and said "that's right, Five ! Always lay the blame on others !"

"You'd better not talk !"said Five, "I

heard the Queen say only yesterday she thought of having you beheaded!"

"What for?" said the one who had spoken first.

"That's not your business, Two!" said Seven.

"Yes, it _is_ his business!" said Five, "and I'll tell him: it was for bringing tulip-roots to the cook instead of potatoes."

Seven flung down his brush, and had just begun "well! Of all the unjust things——" when his eye fell upon Alice, and he stopped suddenly: the others looked round, and all of them took off their hats and bowed low.

"Would you tell me, please," said Alice timidly. "why you are painting those roses?"

Five and Seven looked at Two, but said nothing: Two began, in a low voice, "why, Miss, the fact is, this ought to have been a red rose tree, and we put a white one in by mistake, and if the Queen was to find it out, we should all have our heads cut off. So, you see, we're doing our best, before she comes, to——" At this moment Five, who had been looking anxiously across the garden called out "the Queen! the Queen!" and

the three gardeners instantly threw them-
-selves flat upon their faces. There was a
sound of many footsteps, and Alice looked
round, eager to see the Queen.

First came ten soldiers carrying clubs:
these were all shaped like the three gardeners,
flat and oblong, with their hands and feet at
the corners: next the ten courtiers; these
were all ornamented with diamonds, and
walked two and two, as the soldiers did. After
these came the Royal children: there were ten
of them, and the little dears came jumping
merrily along, hand in hand, in couples: they
were all ornamented with hearts. Next came
the guests, mostly kings and queens, among
whom Alice recognised the white rabbit: it
was talking in a hurried nervous manner,
smiling at everything that was said, and
went by without noticing her. Then followed
the Knave of Hearts, carrying the King's crown
on a cushion, and, last of all this grand pro-
-cession, came THE KING AND QUEEN
OF HEARTS.

When the procession came opposite
to Alice, they all stopped and looked at her, and

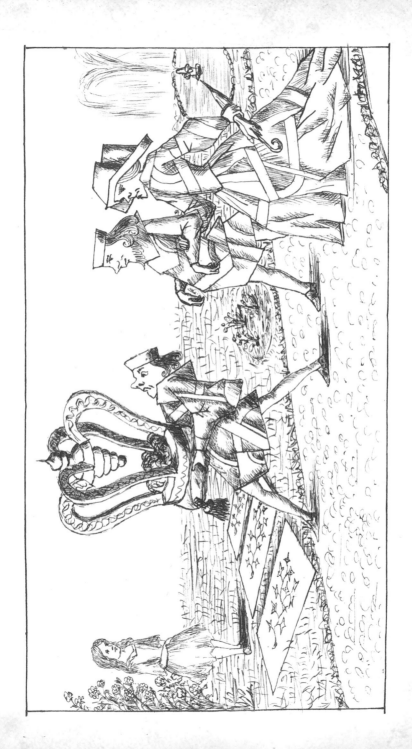

the Queen said severely "who is this?" She said it to the Knave of Hearts, who only bowed and smiled in reply.

"Idiot!" said the Queen, turning up her nose, and asked Alice "what's your name?"

"My name is Alice, so please your Majesty," said Alice boldly, for she thought to herself "why, they're only a pack of cards! I needn't be afraid of them!"

"Who are these?" said the Queen, pointing to the three gardeners lying round the rose tree, for, as they were lying on their faces, and the pattern on their backs was the same as the rest of the pack, she could not tell whether they were gardeners, or soldiers, or courtiers, or three of her own children.

"How should I know?" said Alice, surprised at her own courage, "it's no business of mine."

The Queen turned crimson with fury, and, after glaring at her for a minute, began in a voice of thunder "off with her——"

"Nonsense!" said Alice, very loudly and decidedly, and the Queen was silent.

The King laid his hand upon her arm, and said timidly "remember, my dear! She is only a child!"

The Queen turned angrily away from him, and said to the Knave "turn them over!"

The Knave did so, very carefully, with one foot.

"Get up!" said the Queen, in a shrill loud voice, and the three gardeners instantly jumped up, and began bowing to the King, the Queen, the Royal children, and everybody else.

"Leave off that!" screamed the Queen, "you make me giddy". And then, turning to the rose tree, she went on "what <u>have</u> you been doing here?"

"May it please your Majesty", said Two very humbly, going down on one knee. as he spoke, "we were trying ——"

"<u>I</u> see!" said the Queen, who had meantime been examining the roses, "off with their heads!" and the procession moved on, three of the soldiers remaining behind to execute the three unfortunate gardeners, who ran to Alice for protection.

"You shan't be beheaded!" said Alice, and she put them into her pocket: the three soldiers marched once round her, looking for them, and then quietly marched off after the others.

"Are their heads off?" shouted the Queen.

"Their heads are gone," the soldiers shouted in reply, "if it please your Majesty!"

"That's right!" shouted the Queen, "can you play croquet?"

The soldiers were silent, and looked at Alice, as the question was evidently meant for her.

"Yes!" shouted Alice at the top of her voice.

"Come on then!" roared the Queen, and Alice joined the procession, wondering very much what would happen next.

"It's — its a very fine day!" said a timid little voice: she was walking by the white rabbit, who was peeping anxiously into her face.

"Very," said Alice, "where's the Marchioness?"

"Hush, hush!" said the rabbit in a low voice, "she'll hear you. The Queen's the Marchioness: didn't you know that?"

"No, I didn't," said Alice, "what of?"

"Queen of Hearts," said the rabbit in a whisper, putting its mouth close to her ear, "and Marchioness of Mock Turtles."

"What are _they_?" said Alice, but there was no time for the answer, for they had reached the croquet-ground, and the game began instantly.

Alice thought she had never seen such a curious croquet-ground in all her life: it was all in ridges and furrows: the croquet-balls were live hedgehogs, the mallets live ostriches, and the soldiers had to double themselves up, and stand

on their feet and hands, to make the arches.

The chief difficulty which Alice found at first was to manage her ostrich: she got its body tucked away, comfortably enough, under her arm, with its legs hanging down, but generally, just as she had got its neck straightened out nicely, and was going to give a blow with its head, it _would_ twist itself round, and look up into her face, with such a puzzled expression

that she could not help bursting out laughing: and when she had got its head down, and was going to begin again, it was very confusing to find that the hedgehog had unrolled itself, and was in the act of crawling away: besides all this, there was generally a ridge or a furrow in her way, wherever she wanted to send the hedgehog to, and as the doubled-up soldiers were always getting up and walking off to other parts of the ground, Alice soon came to the conclusion that it was a very difficult game indeed.

The players all played at once without waiting for turns, and quarrelled all the while at the tops of their voices, and in a very few minutes the Queen was in a furious passion, and went stamping about and shouting "off with his head!" or "off with her head!" about once in a minute. All those whom she sentenced were taken into custody by the soldiers, who of course had to leave off being arches to do this, so that, by the end of half an hour or so, there were no arches left, and all the players, except the King, the Queen, and Alice, were in custody, and under sentence of execution.

Then the Queen left off, quite out of breath, and said to Alice "have you seen the Mock Turtle?"

"No," said Alice, "I don't even know what a Mock Turtle is."

"Come on then," said the Queen, "and it shall tell you its history."

As they walked off together, Alice heard the King say in a low voice, to the company generally, "you are all pardoned."

"Come, that's a good thing!" thought Alice, who had felt quite grieved at the number of executions which the Queen had ordered.

They very soon came upon a Gryphon, which lay fast asleep in the sun: (if you don't know what a Gryphon is, look at the picture): "up, lazy thing!" said the Queen, "and take this young lady to see the Mock Turtle, and to

hear its history. I must go back and see after some executions I ordered," and she walked off, leaving Alice with the Gryphon. Alice did not quite like the look of the creature, but on the whole she thought it quite as safe to stay as to go after that savage Queen: so she waited.

The Gryphon sat up and rubbed its eyes: then it watched the Queen till she was out of sight: then it chuckled. "What fun!" said the Gryphon, half to itself, half to Alice.

"What is the fun?" said Alice.

"Why, she," said the Gryphon; "it's all her fancy, that: they never executes nobody, you know: come on!"

"Everybody says 'come on!' here," thought Alice, as she walked slowly after the Gryphon; "I "never was ordered about so before in all my life — never!"

They had not gone far before they saw the Mock Turtle in the distance, sitting sad and lonely on a little ledge of rock, and, as they came nearer, Alice could hear it sighing as if it its heart would break. She pitied it deeply: "what is its sorrow?" she asked the Gryphon, and the Gryphon an- -swered, very nearly in the same words as before," it's all its fancy, that : it hasn't got no sorrow, you know: come on!"

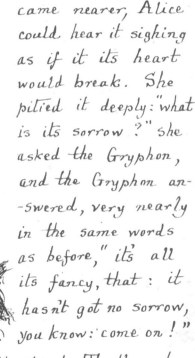

So they went up to the Mock Turtle, who looked at them with large eyes full of tears, but said nothing.

"This here young lady" said the Gryphon,

"wants for to know your history, she do."

"I'll tell it," said the Mock Turtle, in a deep hollow tone, "sit down, and don't speak till I've finished."

So they sat down, and no one spoke for some minutes: Alice thought to herself "I don't see how it can _ever_ finish, if it doesn't begin," but she waited patiently.

"Once," said the Mock Turtle at last, with a deep sigh, "I was a real Turtle."

These words were followed by a very long silence, broken only by an occasional ex--clamation of "hjckrrh!" from the Gryphon, and the constant heavy sobbing of the Mock Turtle. Alice was very nearly getting up and saying, "thank you, sir, for your interesting story," but she could not help thinking there _must_ be more to come, so she sat still and said nothing.

"When we were little," the Mock Turtle went on, more calmly, though still sobbing a little now and then, "we went to school in the sea. The master was an old Turtle — we used to call him Tortoise — "

"Why did you call him Tortoise, if he wasn't one?" asked Alice.

"We called him Tortoise because he taught us," said the Mock Turtle angrily, "really you are very dull!"

"You ought to be ashamed of yourself for asking such a simple question," added the Gryphon, and then they both sat silent and looked at poor Alice, who felt ready to sink into the earth: at last the Gryphon said to the Mock Turtle, "get on, old fellow! Don't be all day!" and the Mock Turtle went on in these words:

"You may not have lived much under the sea—" ("I haven't," said Alice,) "and perhaps you were never even introduced to a lobster—" (Alice began to say "I once tasted—" but hastily checked herself, and said "no, never," instead,) "so you can have no idea what a delightful thing a Lobster Quadrille is!"

"No, indeed," said Alice, "what sort of a thing is it?"

"Why," said the Gryphon, "you form into a line along the sea shore—"

"Two lines!" cried the Mock Turtle, "seals, turtles, salmon, and so on— advance twice—"

"Each with a lobster as partner!" cried the Gryphon.

"Of course," the Mock Turtle said, "advance twice, set to partners —"

"Change lobsters, and retire in same order —" interrupted the Gryphon.

"Then, you know," continued the Mock Turtle, "you throw the —"

"The lobsters!" shouted the Gryphon, with a bound into the air.

"As far out to sea as you can —"

"Swim after them!" screamed the Gryphon.

"Turn a somersault in the sea!" cried the Mock Turtle, capering wildly about.

"Change lobsters again!" yelled the Gryphon at the top of its voice, "and then —"

"That's all," said the Mock Turtle, suddenly dropping its voice, and the two creatures, who had been jumping about like mad things all this time, sat down again very sadly and quietly, and looked at Alice.

"It must be a very pretty dance," said Alice timidly.

"Would you like to see a little of it?" said the Mock Turtle.

"Very much indeed," said Alice.

"Come, let's try the first figure!" said the Mock Turtle to the Gryphon, "we can do it without lobsters, you know. Which shall sing?"

"Oh! you sing!" said the Gryphon, "I've forgotten the words."

So they began solemnly dancing round and round Alice, every now and then treading on her toes when they came too close, and waving their fore-paws to mark the time, while the Mock Turtle sang, slowly and sadly, these words:

"Beneath the waters of the sea
Are lobsters thick as thick can be—
They love to dance with you and me,
    My own, my gentle Salmon!"

The Gryphon joined in singing the chorus, which was:

"Salmon come up! Salmon go down!
Salmon come twist your tail around!
Of all the fishes of the sea
    There's none so good as Salmon!"

"Thank you," said Alice, feeling very glad that the figure was over.

"Shall we try the second figure?" said the Gryphon, "or would you prefer a song?"

"Oh, a song, please!" Alice replied, so eagerly, that the Gryphon said, in a rather offended tone, "hm! no accounting for tastes! Sing her 'Mock Turtle Soup', will you, old fellow!"

The Mock Turtle sighed deeply, and began, in a voice sometimes choked with sobs, to sing this:


"Beautiful Soup, so rich and green,
Waiting in a hot tureen!
Who for such dainties would not stoop?
Soup of the evening, beautiful Soup!
Soup of the evening, beautiful Soup!
    Beau — ootiful   Soo — oop!
    Beau — ootiful   Soo - oop!
Soo - oop of the e- e- evening,
    Beautiful beautiful Soup!


"Chorus again!" cried the Gryphon, and

the Mock Turtle had just begun to repeat it, when a cry of "the trial's beginning!" was heard in the distance.

"Come on!" cried the Gryphon, and, taking Alice by the hand, he hurried off, without waiting for the end of the song.

"What trial is it?" panted Alice as she ran, but the Gryphon only answered "come on!" and ran the faster, and more and more faintly came, borne on the breeze that followed them, the melancholy words:

"Soo—oop of the e—e—evening,
Beautiful beautiful Soup!"

The King and Queen were seated on their throne when they arrived, with a great crowd assembled around them: the Knave was in custody: and before the King stood the white rabbit, with a trumpet in one hand, and a scroll of parchment in the other.

"Herald! read the accusation!" said the King.

On this the white rabbit blew three blasts on the trumpet, and then unrolled the parchment scroll, and read as follows:

"The Queen of Hearts she made some tarts
    All on a summer day:
The Knave of Hearts he stole those tarts,
    And took them quite away!"

"Now for the evidence," said the King, "and
then the sentence."

"No!" said the
Queen, "first the
sentence, and then
the evidence!"

"Nonsense!" cried
Alice, so loudly that
everybody jumped,
"the idea of having
the sentence first!

"Hold your
tongue!" said the Queen.

"I won't!" said Alice, "you're nothing but a
pack of cards! Who cares for you?"

At this the whole pack rose up into the
air, and came flying down upon her: she gave
a little scream of fright, and tried to beat
them off, and found herself lying on the bank,
with her head in the lap of her sister, who was
gently brushing away some leaves that had
fluttered down from the trees on to her face.

"Wake up, Alice dear!" said her sister, "what a nice long sleep you've had!"

"Oh, I've had such a curious dream!" said Alice, and she told her sister all her Adventures Under Ground, as you have read them, and when she had finished, her sister kissed her and said "it _was_ a curious dream, dear, certainly! But now run in to your tea: it's getting late."

So Alice ran off, thinking while she ran (as well she might) what a wonderful dream it had been.

---

But her sister sat there some while longer, watching the setting sun, and thinking of little Alice and her Adventures, till she too began dreaming after a fashion, and this was her dream:

She saw an ancient city, and a quiet river winding near it along the plain, and up the stream went slowly gliding a boat with a merry party of children on board — she could hear their voices and laughter like music over the water — and among them was another little Alice, who sat listening with bright eager eyes to a tale that was being told, and she listened for the words of the tale, and lo! it was the dream of her own little sister. So the boat wound slowly along, beneath the bright summer-day, with its merry crew and its music of voices and laughter, till it passed round one of the many turnings of the stream, and she saw it no more.

Then she thought, (in a dream within the dream, as it were,) how this same little Alice would, in the after-time, be herself a grown woman: and how she would keep, through her riper years, the simple and loving heart of her childhood: and how she would gather around her other little children, and make their eyes bright and eager with many a wonderful tale, perhaps even with these very adventures of the little Alice of long-ago: and how she would feel with all their simple sorrows, and find a pleasure in all their simple joys, remembering her own child-life, and the happy summer-days.